AF270659

NFL TEAMS

MINNESOTA VIKINGS

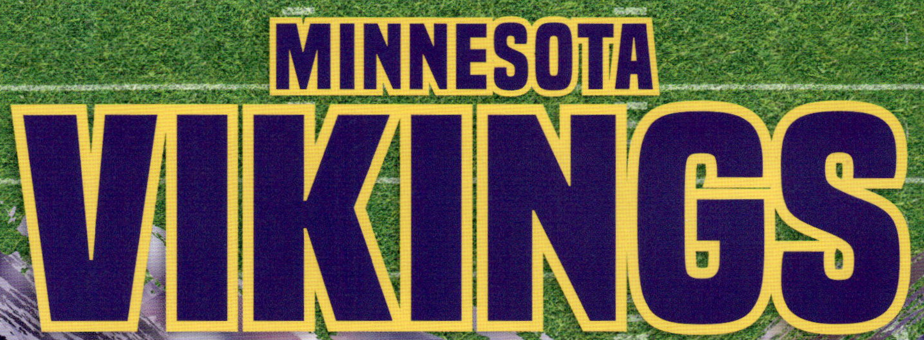

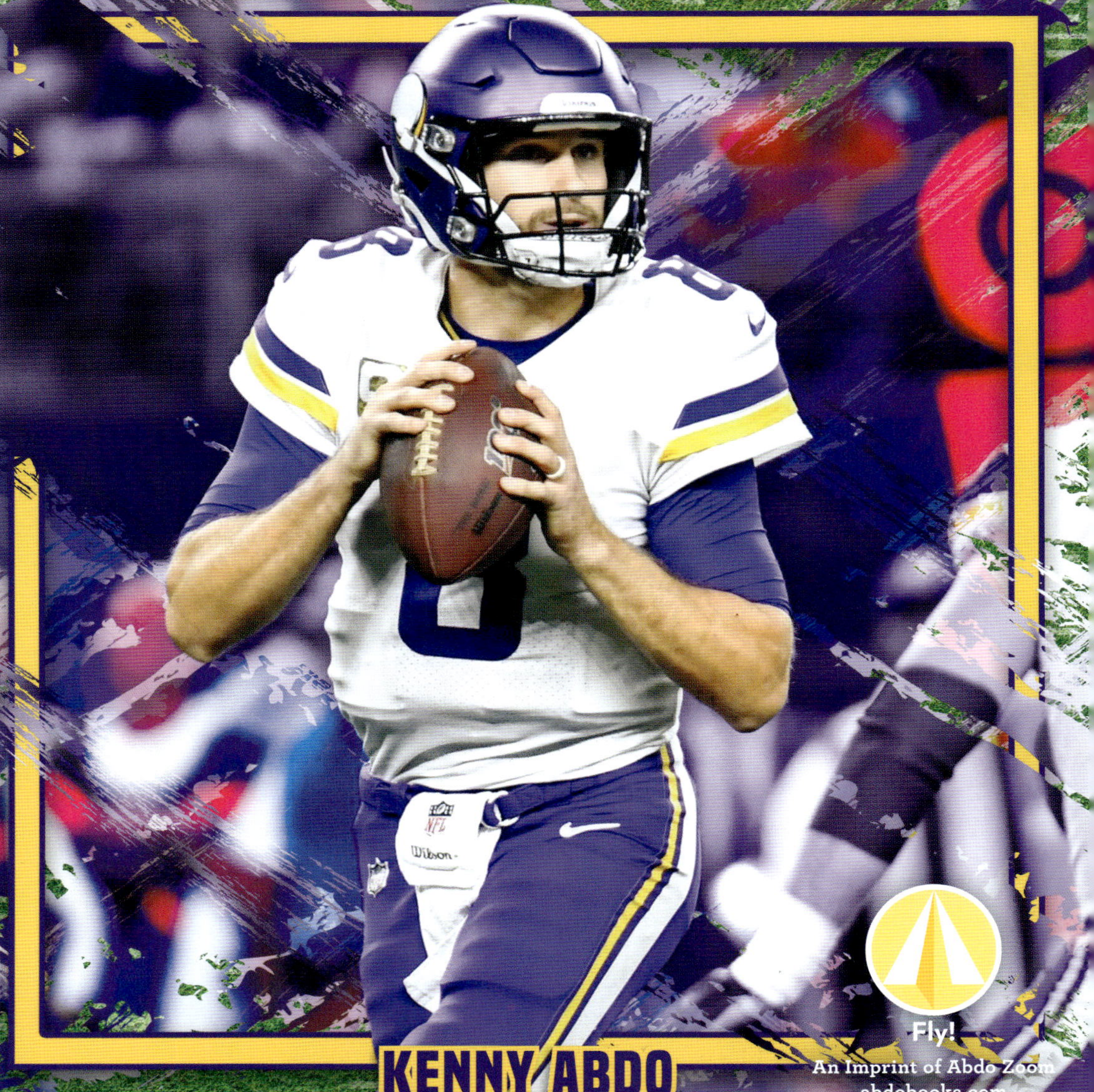

KENNY ABDO

Fly!
An Imprint of Abdo Zoom
abdobooks.com

abdobooks.com

Published by Abdo Zoom, a division of ABDO, P.O. Box 398166, Minneapolis, Minnesota 55439. Copyright © 2022 by Abdo Consulting Group, Inc. International copyrights reserved in all countries. No part of this book may be reproduced in any form without written permission from the publisher. Fly!™ is a trademark and logo of Abdo Zoom.
Printed in China
052021
092021

Photo Credits: AP Images, Getty Images, Icon Sportswire, iStock, Shutterstock PREMIER
Production Contributors: Kenny Abdo, Jennie Forsberg, Grace Hansen
Design Contributors: Candice Keimig, Neil Klinepier

Library of Congress Control Number: 2020919710

Publisher's Cataloging-in-Publication Data

Names: Abdo, Kenny, author.
Title: Minnesota Vikings / by Kenny Abdo
Description: Minneapolis, Minnesota : Abdo Zoom, 2022 | Series: NFL teams |
    Includes online resources and index.
Identifiers: ISBN 9781098224714 (lib. bdg.) | ISBN 9781098225650 (ebook) |
    ISBN 9781098226121 (Read-to-Me ebook)
Subjects: LCSH: Minnesota Vikings (Football team)--Juvenile literature. | National
    Football League--Juvenile literature. | Football teams--Juvenile literature. |
    American football--Juvenile literature. | Professional sports--Juvenile literature.
Classification: DDC 796.33264--dc23

TABLE OF CONTENTS

MINNESOTA VIKINGS

Battling for wins and plundering the football field, the Minnesota Vikings fight hard against their opponents.

With **Super Bowl** appearances and miracles performed, fans will be chanting their signature battle-cry "skol" for years to come!

ank stadium
PENTAIR
20
MACKENSIE
ALEXANDER
CORNERBACK
25
WATS
Andersen

KICK OFF

The Vikings were founded by a group
of five businessmen in 1960. The team's
first game was against the Chicago
Bears in 1961. The Vikings won 37–13!

The Vikings got their first **division** title in 1968 after beating the Philadelphia Eagles 24-17. It sent the team to the playoffs, only to lose to the Baltimore Colts 24-14.

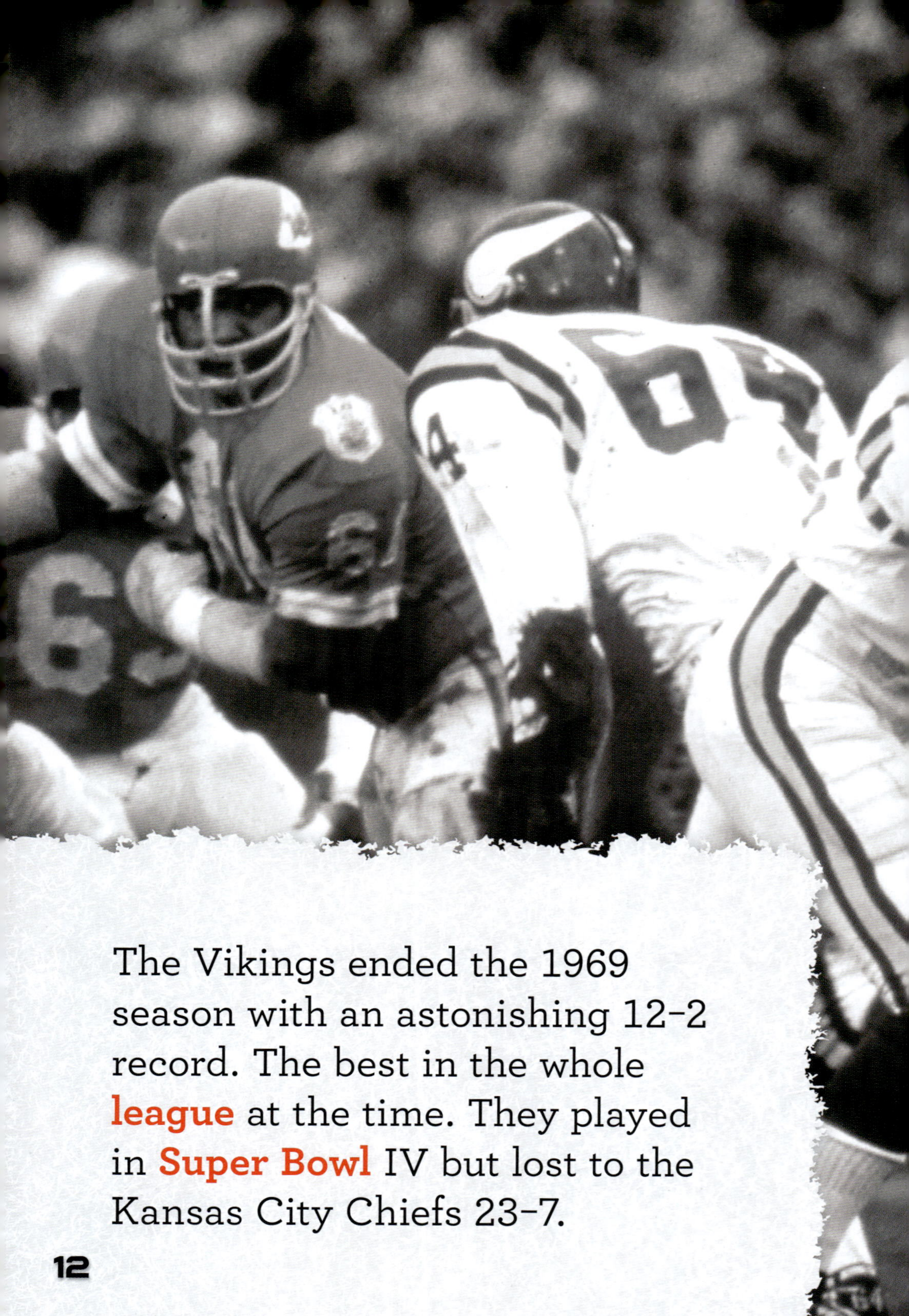

The Vikings ended the 1969 season with an astonishing 12-2 record. The best in the whole **league** at the time. They played in **Super Bowl** IV but lost to the Kansas City Chiefs 23-7.

TEAM RECAPS

The Vikings defense was so strong in the 1970s they earned the nickname the "Purple People Eaters." The team made appearances in **Super Bowl** VIII, IX, and XI. Unfortunately, the Vikes never walked away with a victory.

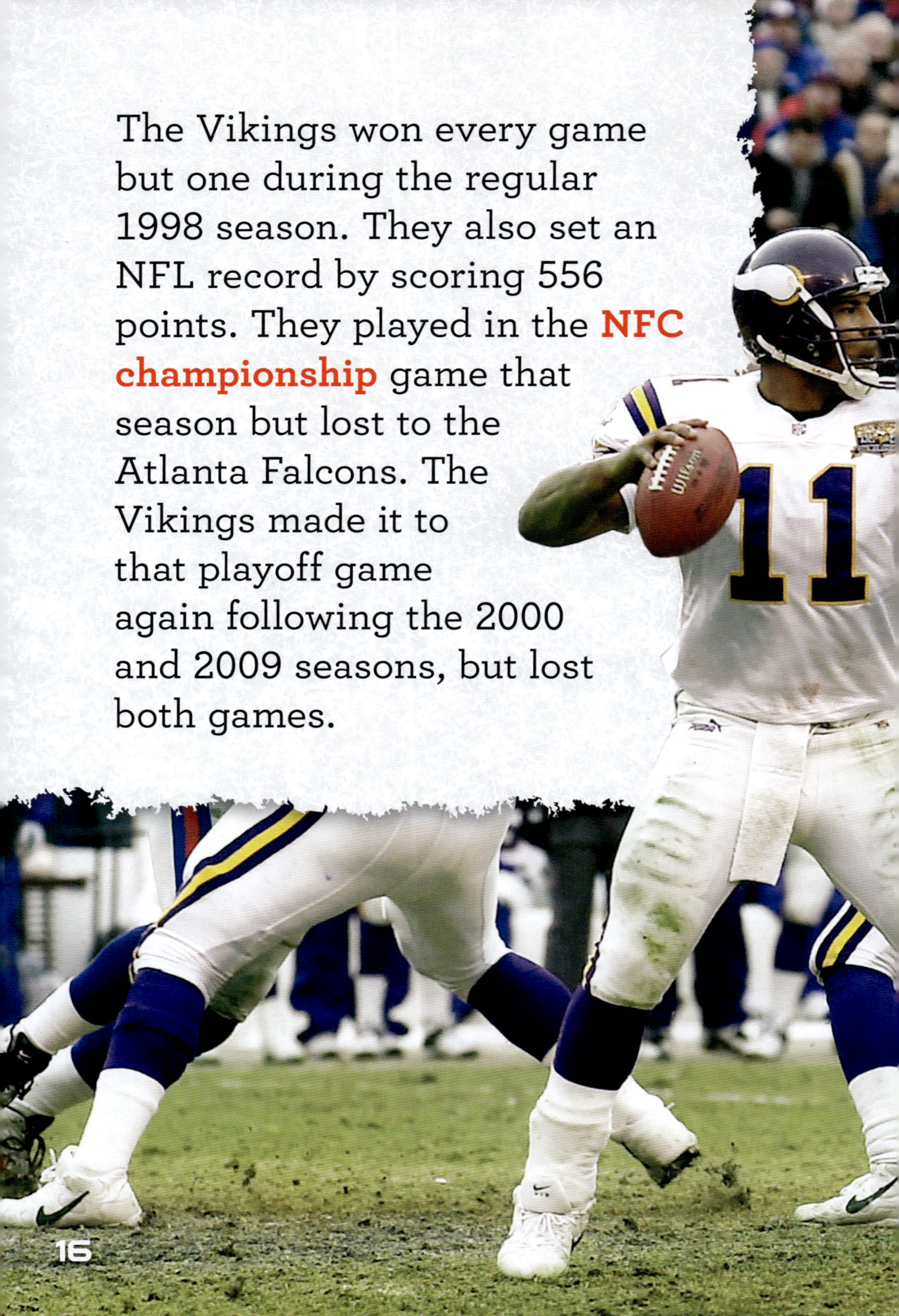

The Vikings won every game but one during the regular 1998 season. They also set an NFL record by scoring 556 points. They played in the **NFC championship** game that season but lost to the Atlanta Falcons. The Vikings made it to that playoff game again following the 2000 and 2009 seasons, but lost both games.

STRAHAN
92
71

In the last 10 seconds of the 2017 **divisional** playoff game, Stefon Diggs caught a 27-yard pass and ran it 34 yards for a touchdown. The play known as the "Minneapolis Miracle" clinched a Vikings win, 29-24, against the Saints.

Kirk Cousins joined the Vikings during the 2018 season. The next season, they made it to the **Wild Card** Playoffs against the Saints. The Vikings won in **overtime** 26–20!

The Vikings ended the 2020 season with a 7-9 record, not qualifying for playoffs. However, the team had nabbed some solid picks in the draft, making the future look a little brighter.

HALL OF FAME

QB Fran Tarkenton helped the Vikings reach the **Super Bowl** three times. Tarkenton had 33,098 passing yards with the team, which is a Vikings record! Tarkenton was **inducted** into the Pro Football Hall of Fame in 1986.

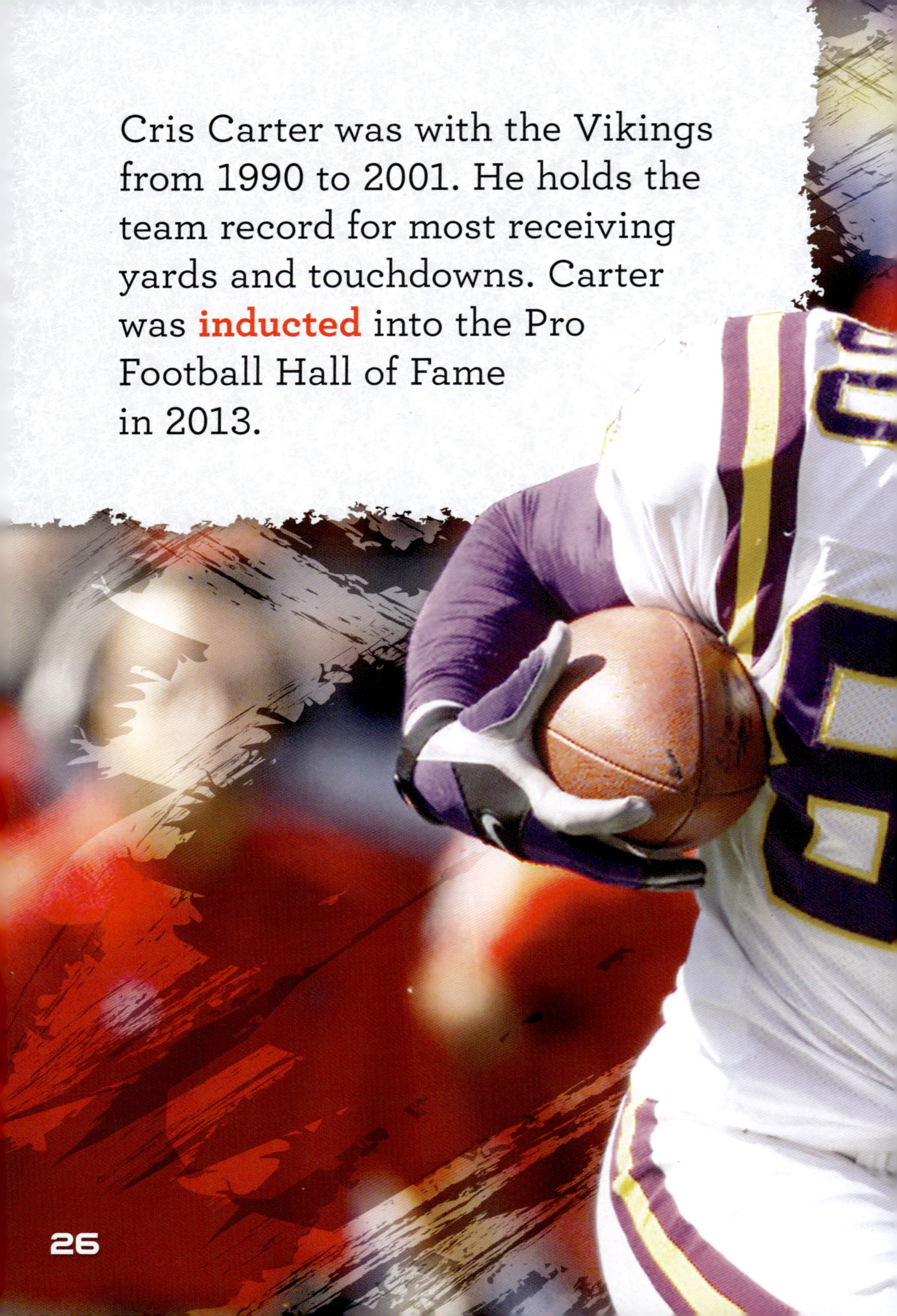

Cris Carter was with the Vikings from 1990 to 2001. He holds the team record for most receiving yards and touchdowns. Carter was **inducted** into the Pro Football Hall of Fame in 2013.

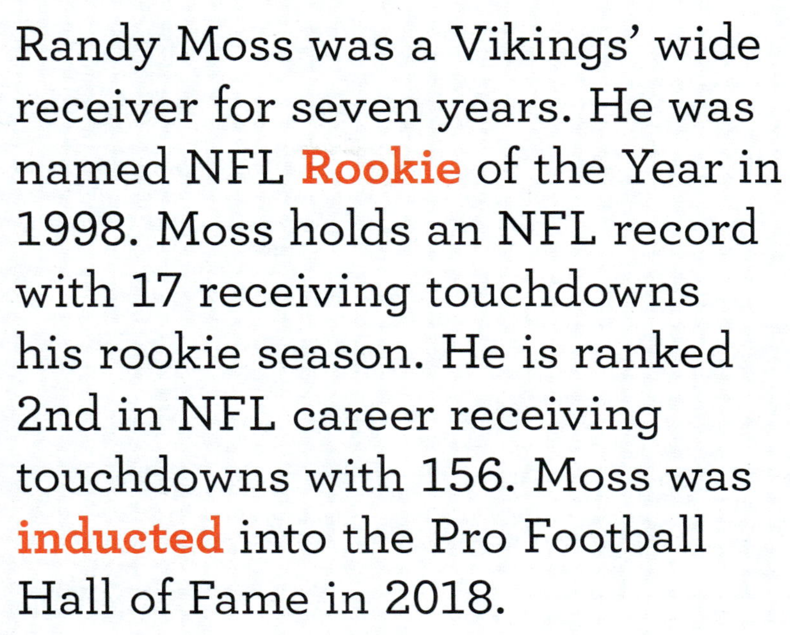

Randy Moss was a Vikings' wide receiver for seven years. He was named NFL **Rookie** of the Year in 1998. Moss holds an NFL record with 17 receiving touchdowns his rookie season. He is ranked 2nd in NFL career receiving touchdowns with 156. Moss was **inducted** into the Pro Football Hall of Fame in 2018.

GLOSSARY

championship – a game held to find a first-place winner.

division – a group of teams who compete against each other for a championship.

induct – to admit someone as a member of an organization.

league – a group of teams that compete against each other.

National Football Conference (NFC) – one of two major conferences of the NFL. Each conference contains 16 teams split into four divisions. The winner of the NFC championship plays the AFC winner at the Super Bowl.

overtime – additional minutes added to a tied-up game giving each team a chance to win.

quarterback (QB) – the player on the offensive team that directs teammates in their play.

rookie – a first-year player in a professional sport.

Super Bowl – the NFL championship game, played once a year.

Wild Card Round – the first round of the playoffs. Each of the two conferences send four division champions and three wild-card teams to its postseason.

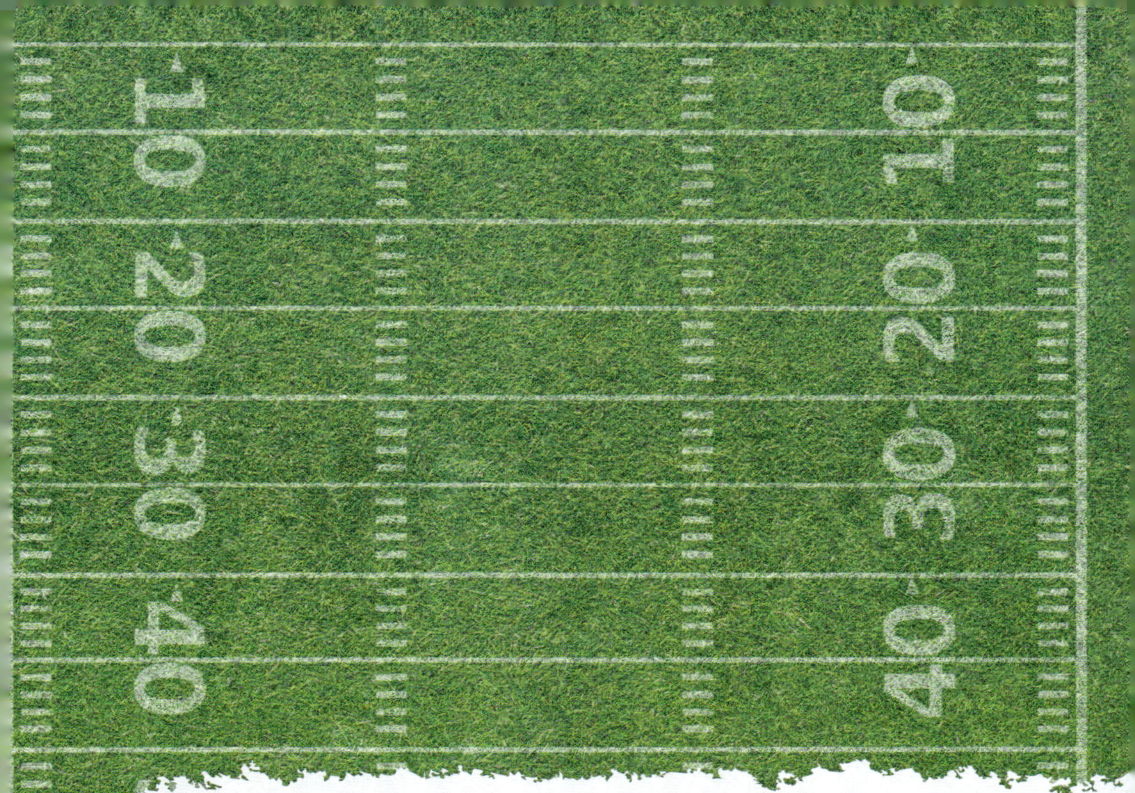

ONLINE RESOURCES

To learn more about the Minnesota Vikings, please visit **abdobooklinks.com** or scan this QR code. These links are routinely monitored and updated to provide the most current information available.

INDEX